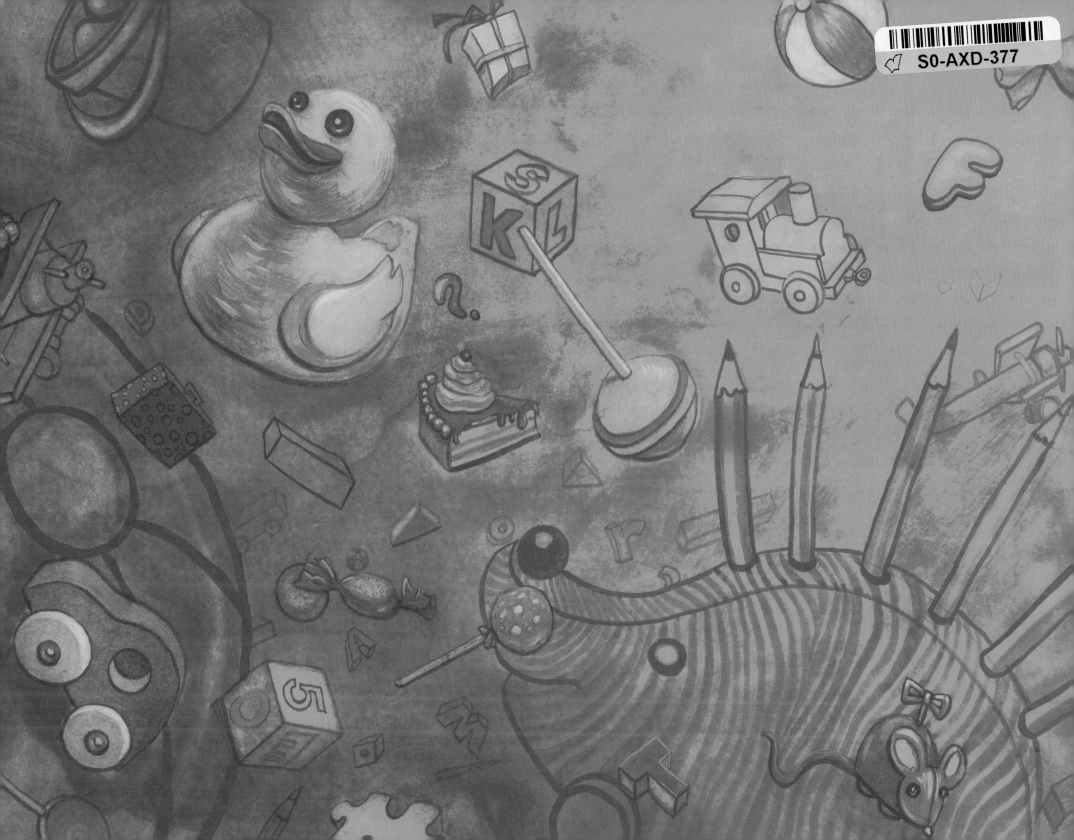

This book belongs to

Happy

To my little friend Tobias, the enthusiastic and clever boy, who inspired me to write books about Happy Toby, and show people where to find happiness in life.

Special thanks to Frantiska, Sylvia, Michael, and Nadia for always supporting my passion to pursue my dreams.

J.K.

HAPPY TOBY

Illustrated stories about a happy childhood

Illustrations by Marek Mertinko
Graphic design by Jitka Janeckova
Deva Ideal typeface by DizajnDesign
Library of Congress Control Number: 2015900764
HAPPY TOBY – Toby and His Family/Jozef Krivicka
Printed in Slovakia
Summary: In the illustrated stories about his childhood,
Toby shows us where to find happiness.

**HAPPY TOBY
PUBLISHING**

TOBY AND HIS FAMILY

Written by Jozef Krivicka

Illustrated by Marek Mertinko

Toby is a preschool boy.
He loves all of his many toys.

Toby's biggest love is his family,
Mom, Dad,
and little sister Emily.

There is also kitty Sissy in
the house,
Toby's buddy and nightmare
of every mouse.

Playing with Emily and Sissy
never ends.
The three together have lots
of fun and are close friends.

Toby's grandparents speed
along the way,
eager to visit their family on
Thanksgiving Day.

Toby welcomes grandma and
grandpa with open arms.
They brought toys and delicious
produce from their farm.

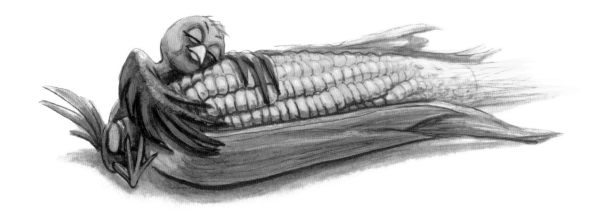

Unloading the truck, Toby is
very handy.
As a reward, he gets
grandma's baked goods and
his favorite candy.

For Toby, grandma is the
world's best cook.
He laughs out loud every time
she reads a story book.

Grandpa fulfills Toby's
longtime wish.
He shows him how to
catch a fish.

Spirits at Thanksgiving dinner are high.
Everybody praises mom's turkey,
cranberries, and pumpkin pie.

This festive time is priceless
for Toby and Emily.
Young and old, all together,
are a happy family.

This is not THE END!

For more stories about Happy Toby please go to

www.HappyToby.com

JOZEF KRIVICKA, the author of this book was born in Czechoslovakia. After studying acting at the Academy of Performing Arts in Bratislava, Slovakia, he was featured in a number of productions in the Theater for Children and Youth, as well as in TV productions for children. He emigrated from communist Czechoslovakia to West Germany in 1986. Jozef moved to the USA in 1997, and studied English at the International College in Naples, Florida, where he lives with his wife Frantiska. He has two children, Michael and Sylvia, and two grandsons, Ethan and Miles.

MAREK MERTINKO graduated from the Academy of Fine Arts in Bratislava, Slovakia. He has a master's degree in illustration and printmaking. His work is a symbiosis of his talent, humor, and unique point of view, as well as a respectable art style.